LITTLE LOUIE
TAKES OFF

For my parents and in memory of my grandfather,
Oscar Morison, an early aviator

First published in the United States of America in 2007 by
Walker Publishing Company, Inc.
Distributed to the trade by Holtzbrinck Publishers
First published in Great Britain in 2007 by Simon & Schuster UK Ltd

For information about permission to reproduce selections from
this book, write to Permissions, Walker & Company,
104 Fifth Avenue, New York, New York 10011

Library of Congress Cataloging-in-Publication Data
Morison, Toby.
Little Louie takes off / Toby Morison.
p.   cm.
Summary: Little Louie must take a plane south for the winter because he has not yet
learned to fly, but he becomes lonely while waiting for his family, and the desire for a friend,
combined with an accident, provides the motivation he needs to trust his wings.
ISBN-13: 978-0-8027-9645-5 • ISBN-10: 0-8027-9645-1 (hardcover)
[1. Flight—Fiction. 2. Birds—Fiction. 3. Loneliness—Fiction.] I. Title.
PZ7.M8267483Lit 2007   [E]—dc22   2006031295

The text for this book is set in Bodoni
The illustrations for this book were rendered in watercolor
Book designed by Genevieve Webster

Visit Walker & Company's Web site at www.walkeryoungreaders.com

Printed in China

2 4 6 8 10 9 7 5 3 1

LITTLE LOUIE
TAKES OFF

TOBY MORISON

WALKER & COMPANY  NEW YORK

Little Louie had still not learned to fly.

"Come on, you can do it!" cheered his brothers and sisters.

"I'm trying," he sighed.

But he just couldn't get the hang of it.

Louie always felt much chirpier playing
hopscotch or flying his kite.

His favorite hobby of all was plane-spotting.
With his binoculars, Louie studied the airplanes
as they soared gracefully in the sky, and he kept
a record of them all in a special spiral-bound
notebook.

As winter approached, his family prepared to fly south for their vacation in the sun. Before they left, they took Louie to the airport.

"I don't want to go alone," Louie sniffled. "I want to go with you!"

"Too bad you can't fly like normal birds," muttered his father.

"Come on, sweetie, don't flap," said his mother. "Going by plane will be very exciting, and we'll see you very soon!"

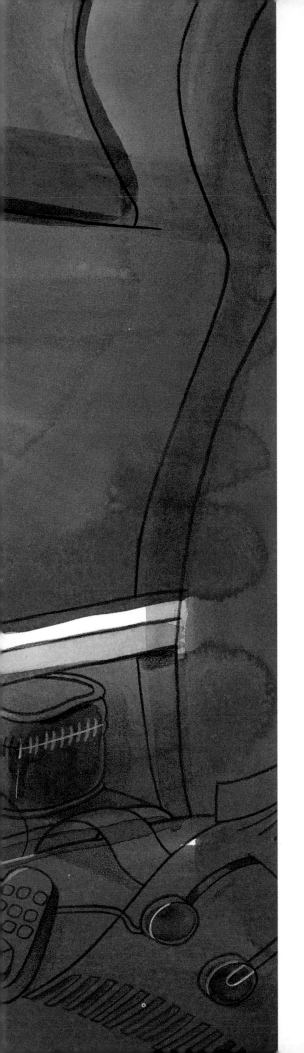

Once the plane took off, Louie nibbled a few peanuts, then nestled against the pillow and drifted off to sleep. He dreamed he could fly.

When the plane landed, Louie woke with a start. "That was a little bumpy," he thought, but he was too polite to mention it, especially because he couldn't fly himself.

"Hello, birdie! I am Miguel," said a flamingo in a heavy accent. "I will take you to your hotel. *Vámonos!*"

When they arrived, Louie looked up at the hotel rooftop. He was tired and he missed his family.

"I want my mommy," he said in a shaky voice.

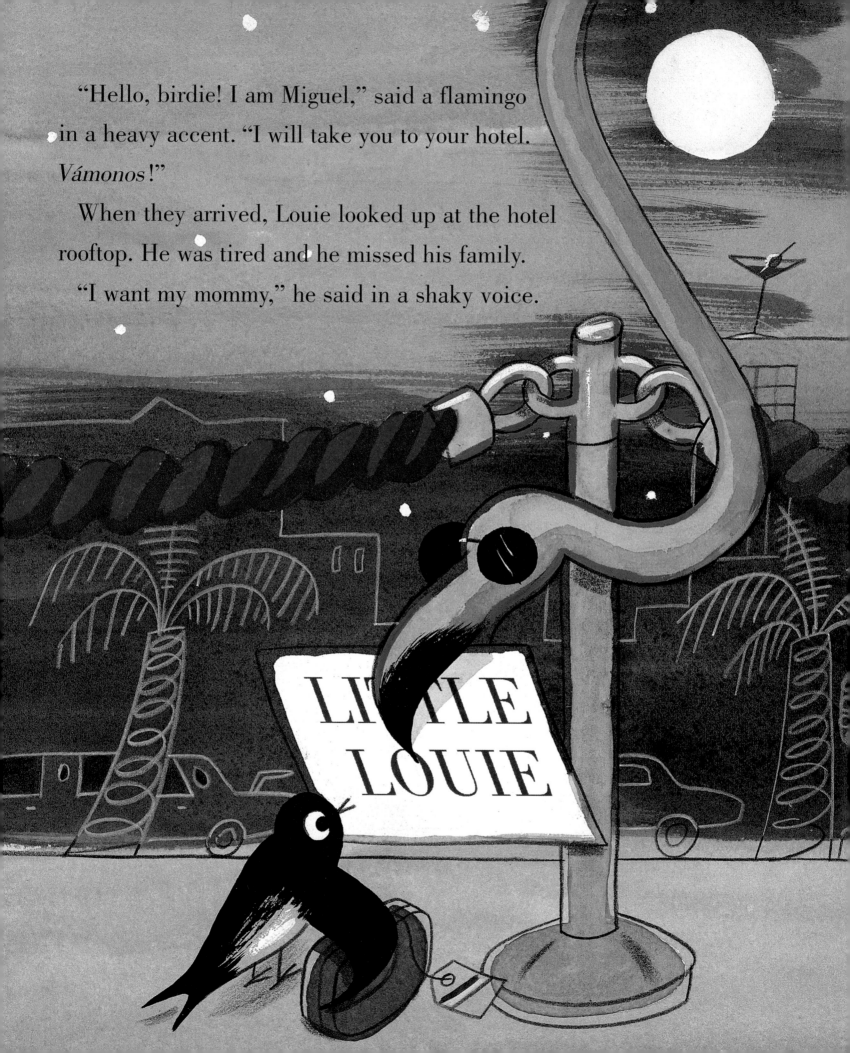

LITTLE LOUIE

"You will wait a long time, *mi amigo*," said Miguel. "Too bad you cannot fly."

It was a long hop up to the rooftop for Louie's tiny legs, but at last he was there. Little Louie fell asleep right away.

In the morning, Louie woke up feeling utterly alone. First, he checked that his return plane ticket was safe.

Then he opened his suitcase and gave himself a good preening.

Louie picked up his binoculars and scanned the skies, looking desperately for his family. There was no sign of them.

That night he cried himself to sleep.

The next day, Louie spotted a penguin standing alone on a rock, folding and throwing paper airplanes. Louie longed to join in and make a friend.

As he was watching the penguin, his plane ticket was picked up by the breeze. . . It caught his eye as it fluttered off the roof.

Without thinking, Louie swooped after it!

Help!

He was falling . . .

plummeting
to the ground
in a tailspin . . .

Mayday!
Mayday!

Louie
swallowed
hard . . .

. . . then suddenly he felt his wing tips lift,
and he began to climb.

Louie plucked the ticket from the air and
soared into the glorious blue sky.

He was flying!

From high above, Little Louie saw the penguin!
He swooped down and landed with a bump.

"Hello!" said the penguin. "My name's Gwynn."

Louie told Gwynn all about the airplane, the ticket,
and how much he missed his family.

"Oh, don't worry," said Gwynn kindly. "It's just that
birds fly much more slowly than airplanes. But if you
ever feel lonely, you're always welcome here."

Louie flew down to see Gwynn every day. They soon became best friends, talking for hours about all the places they'd like to see.

"But I'll never be able to go to any of these places," sighed Gwynn. "You see, penguins can't fly—we're too heavy and our wings aren't big enough."

Louie felt sorry for Gwynn. He wished there was something he could do to help.

Then, one happy morning, Little Louie's family finally flew into view. He had a surprise ready for them.

"Bravo to our little high-flyer!" they cried.

"I'm very proud of you," said his father, giving him a hug.

Louie's chest swelled. "Oh, it was a breeze," he said airily.

Reunited at last, the family enjoyed a wonderful vacation together. Little Louie took them all to meet Gwynn, who showed them how to make paper airplanes.

Time flew by, and soon the day came for Louie to say farewell to his special friend. He gave Gwynn a big hug and handed him a long envelope . . .

Louie's family was ready to leave.

"Now don't fly too fast," they warned. "It's going to be a long haul!"

But Louie had more important things on his mind when he took to the skies.

As a plane flew past, he urgently scanned the windows. His wings beat faster in delight as he recognized, in seat 17E, a first-time flyer.

Gwynn grinned and waved.

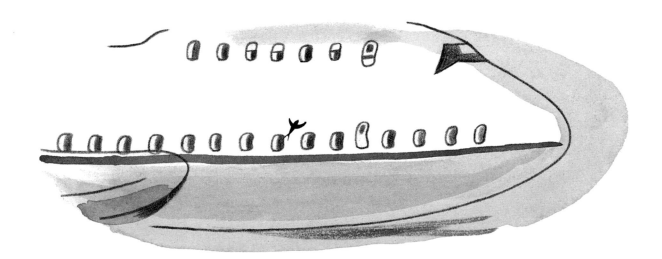

Louie smiled and swooped to join his family
in formation as they headed for home.